Mordecai Cubitt Cooke, Edward Bury

Polycystins, Figures of Remarkable Forms &c.

in the Barbados chalk deposit (chiefly collected by Dr. Davy, and noticed in

a lecture delivered to the Agricultural Society of Barbados, in July, 1846)

Mordecai Cubitt Cooke, Edward Bury

Polycystins, Figures of Remarkable Forms &c.
in the Barbados chalk deposit (chiefly collected by Dr. Davy, and noticed in a lecture delivered to the Agricultural Society of Barbados, in July, 1846)

ISBN/EAN: 9783337403454

Printed in Europe, USA, Canada, Australia, Japan

Cover: Foto ©Andreas Hilbeck / pixelio.de

More available books at **www.hansebooks.com**

POLYCYSTINS,

FIGURES OF REMARKABLE FORMS &c.,

IN THE

BARBADOS CHALK DEPOSIT,

(Chiefly collected by Dr. Davy, and noticed in a Lecture delivered to the Agricultural Society of Barbados, in July, 1846.)

DRAWN BY MRS. BURY,

As seen in her Microscope, on Slides prepared by Chr. Johnson, Esq., of Lancaster, 1860 and 1861.

SECOND EDITION,

EDITED BY M. C. COOKE.

PUBLISHED BY W. WHELDON, 58, GREAT QUEEN STREET, LONDON. W.C.

NOTICE TO SECOND EDITION.

The 'negatives' of this work and all interest and copyright having passed into my hands, I have, in consequence of numerous demands for copies resolved upon the reissue of the entire work, as originally published—so that all references and quotations heretofore made to plates, figures, or descriptions will equally apply to the present, which I trust will be found in no way inferior to the first edition.

M. C. C.

POLYCYSTINS.

—

PREFACE TO FIRST EDITION.

"BUT WHAT ARE POLYCYSTINS" is the constant exclamation.—So little is yet known of these curious organisms that naturalists have not yet decided on their exact place. They belong however, to the sub-kingdom "PROTOZOA," and Mr. Reay Greene in his "Manual" places them between "RHIZOPODA" (of which the type is *Amœba*, so commonly found in fresh water as little gelatinous lumps, of the very lowest form of animal life) and SPONGES, which form flinty interior skeletons, called spicules, to support the spongiose web, and the animal mass of jelly, called SARCODE, with which they are invested. The *Polycystins* are also masses of *Sarcode*, but they appear to form both internal spicular-like supports radiating from the nucleus, and also external shells of a network of flint, through the interstices of which they are said to protrude pseudopodian threads (perhaps analogous to the tentacles of Sea-anemones and Star-fishes or arms of Hydra) by means of which they are supposed to imbibe nourishment, and to have some powers of locomotion. A careful observation of the larval changes of the Echinoderms, and the pupæ states of other young things, can make one understand how the protean forms of the Polycystins need not all designate distinct species, but that many grotesque differences of shape, and of spinous ornamentation may, in reality belong to the same object, in different stages or under different circumstances of development, such as more or less pressure, abundance or scarcity of the siliceous material in the surrounding water, &c. Perhaps there may be said to be four classes of form:—1st., the discoidal or planorbian flattened spheres, variously winged or bordered; 2nd., the orbicular, with or without spines; 3rd., the vase or bell-shaped consisting often of repeated globes growing out of each other, sometimes with a re-duplication of parts, that might seem to indicate a tendency towards increase by fission; 4th., the plane or straight-sided forms.

Dr. Wallich promises a full history of the structure and mode of development of Polycystins in his forthcoming work, having obtained living specimens in his recent deep-sea soundings: some in association with those wondrous benighted star-fishes from two miles deep.

Professor Johannes Müller fished them up frequently in the Mediterranean, near Cette and St. Tropez; always from great depths, and under very clear pure sea-water, but from their great delicacy it was most difficult to obtain really *living* subjects, as even the passing through the water, in hauling up the apparatus used in dredging them caused death, and when that occurred the pseudopodia immediately collapsed, the sarcode substance became flaccid, and little more of the vital economy of the organisms could be observed.

The late Professor W. J. Bailey also records some specimens as occurring among his deep-sea soundings in the Sea of Kamschatka; he speaks of their "organic contents" but does not state whether obtained in a living state.

In the stomachs of the Salpæ, which form so large a portion of the food of whales, shoals of Polycystins are found, which have in their turn served as food to the Salpæ. In a fossil state Polycystins have been found in many parts of the world; those figured in the accompanying Monograph, are from a sort of chalky earth found in various localities in Barbados, where Sir Robert Schomburgk describes it as having been forced up by volcanic action, through the coral reefs of which the island is formed, from the deep bottom of some ancient ocean, where countless ages ago they may have enjoyed their gift of the power of abstracting pure Silex from the water, and, while in a plastic state, weaving it into their elegant glass corslets,—then laying down their skeletons to form part of that incalculably vast bed of ocean-deposits, of which some infinitesimally small fraction occasionally comes under the microscopic ken of man, —to shew us how the minutest and humblest atoms have yet their allotted part in fulfilling the Laws of the Great Creator.

Professor Ehrenberg, in a discourse delivered before the Berlin Royal Academy of Sciences, says, speaking of these fossils from the rocks of Barbados (which he calls *Siliceous Polygastrica*) "for these organisms constitute part of a chain which, though in the individual link it be microscopic, yet in the mass is a mighty one, connecting the *Life-phenomena* of distant ages of the earth, and proving that the dawn of organic nature co-existent with us, reaches farther back in the history of the earth than had hitherto been suspected. The microscopic organisms are very inferior in individual energy to lions and elephants, but in their united influences they are far more important than all these animals."

Professor Owen (in his "Palæontology," 1862,) further remarks "if it ever be permitted to man to penetrate the mystery which enshrouds the origin of organic force in the wide-spread mud beds of fresh and salt waters, it will be, most probably, by experiment and observation on the atoms which manifest the simplest conditions of life."

P. S. B.

Croft Lodge,
January, 1862.

ما .   ٢

PLATE I.

FIG.
1 & 6.—Varieties of Eucyrtidium Acuminatum of Ehrenberg.

5.—Podocyrtis Schomburgkii.   Ehrenberg.

2, 3, 4.—Varieties of the same.

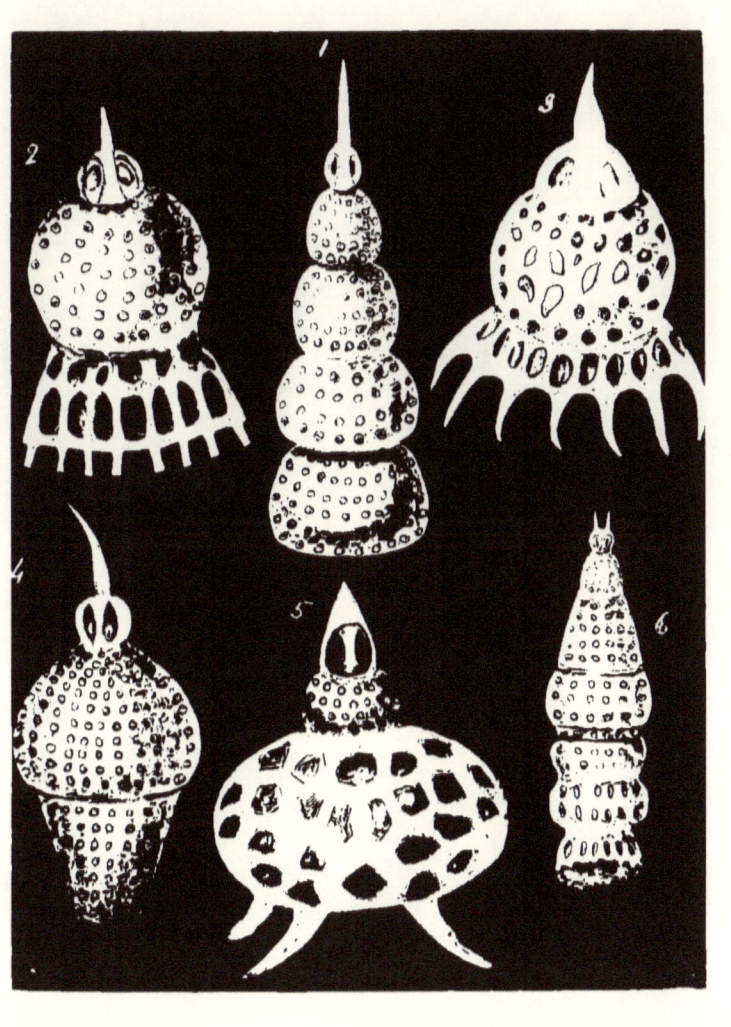

٢
١

PLATE II.

FIG.

1.—Stylodictya gracilis. Ehrenberg.

2.—A Dictyospiris (?) of Ehrenberg, highly developed in slide Z¹⁴⁵, Cambridge, Barbados.

3.—Dictyospiris (?) or perhaps Petalospiris (?) May they not possibly be the same organisms in different states of development? Ceratospiris, (Mikrogeologie, Pl. XXII, fig. 37,) also resembles these shapes which occur in great variety in the Barbados deposits.

4.—Rhabdolithes pipa, spined stem var. Ehrenberg places Rhabdolithes in the family of Geolithen.

5.—Stephanolithes nodosa.; also a Geolithen of Ehrenberg.

6.—Acanthodesmia of J. Müller (Mittelmeeres, p. 30) Stephanolithes spinescens (?) of Ehrenberg. It occurs in double and single circlets, and with varying number of spines in the Barbados deposits.

PLATE III.

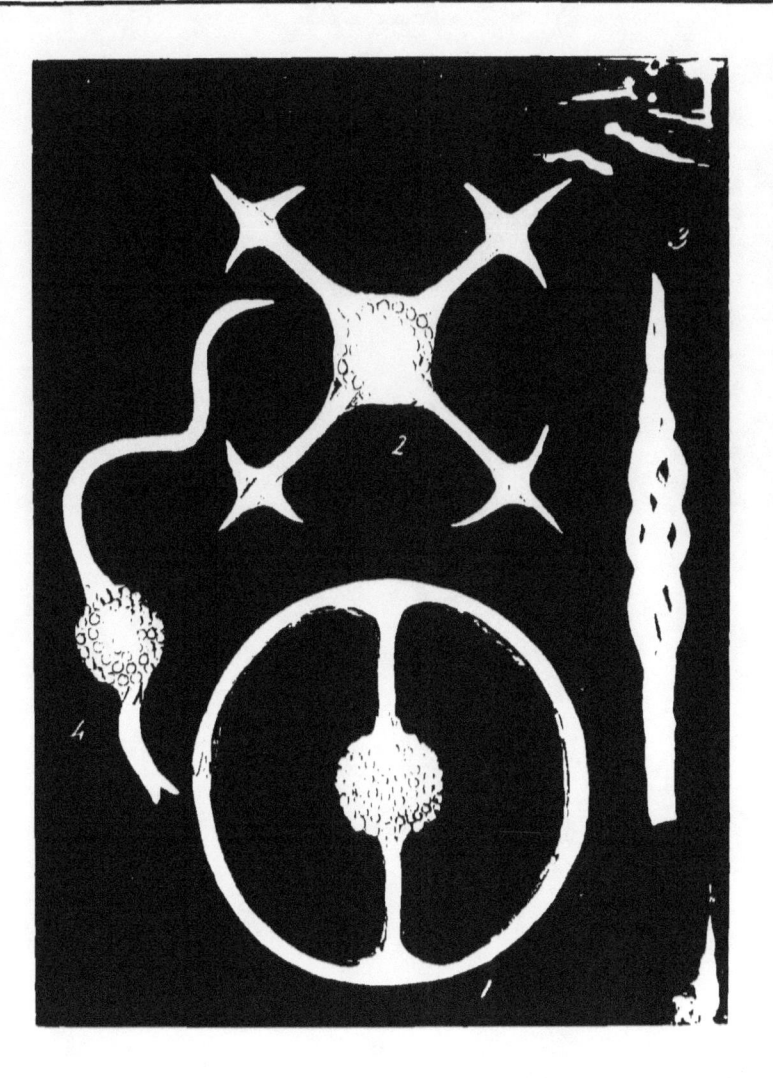

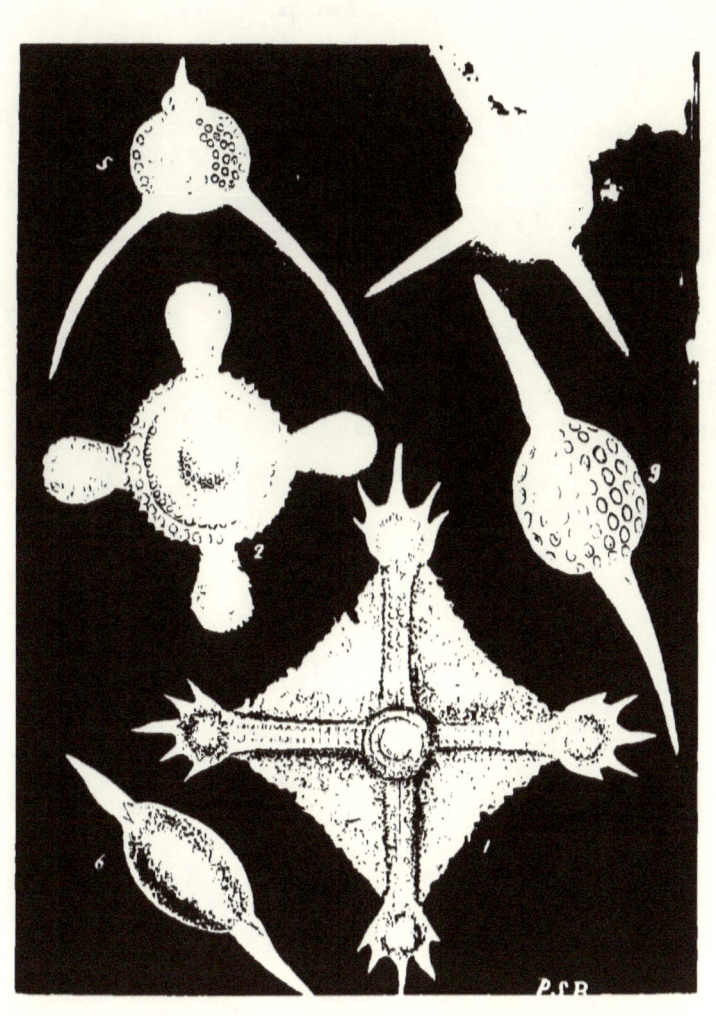

PLATE V.

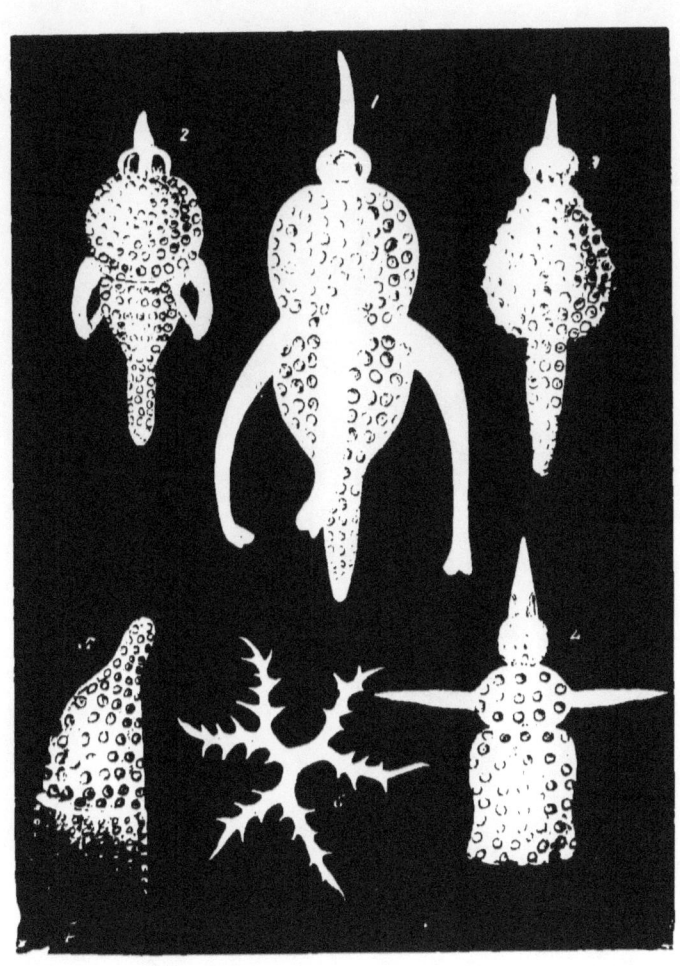

PLATE VII.

FIG.

1 & 2.—Surirella (?) from Cambridge, Barbados. Fig. 1 possibly a young, less developed, form of fig. 2. The slide from which the fig. 2 was drawn was returned to Mr. Johnson, and by him sent to Mr. Ralfs. Professor W. C. Williamson saw it when in Mrs. Bury's hands (October, 1860,) and kindly suggested it might possibly be a Surirella.

3 & 4.—Varieties of Dictyospiris (?) Ehrenberg.

5.—Actiniscus (?) of Ehrenberg and Pritchard; a triangular net, like a Dictyocha, but with a "solid centre," which centre (or nucleus) gives the idea of being capable of stretching up into a Podocyrtis-like form; sides of triangle measure .0065; there are nine outer and six inner cells, arranged round a solid-lobed and punctured nucleus, which bears one long and two short spines.

6.—A Desmidia-like, but silicious, clear, transparent plate, with waved edges, and a perforated centre. Appears to resemble in some degree, Lithodesmium undulatum, of Ehrenberg's "Kreidebildung," page 76. Dr. Wallich suggested (from sketch) that it might be a *part* only of some polycystinous form.

7.—The upper part like Ehrenberg's Podocyrtis cothurnata, but with a tubulous prolongation of the base.

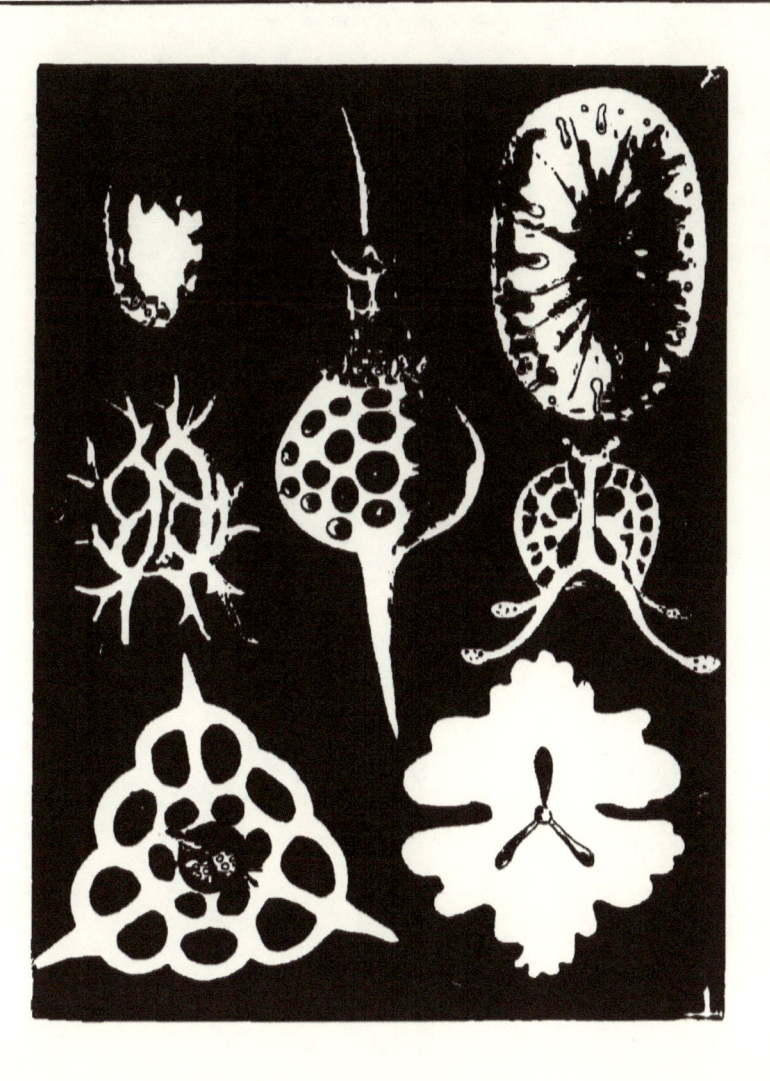

PLATE VIII.

FIG.

1, 2, 3, & 4.—Varieties of Haliomma. Haliomma Humboldtii (?) of
Ehrenberg, from Cambridge, Barbados, numerous and variable.
Although there are sometimes indications of spines radiating
from the centre, as in Stylodictya, yet the points round the edge
appear to be merely "marginal appendages."—Diameters, in-
cluding spines, from .0077 to .0085.

5, & 6.—Müller describes these as stages of growth of the Haliomma,
where the outer web is spinning itself over and round the central
nucleus, and the siliceous rafters or supports extending like a
framework from the nucleus to the exterior covering. (Page 21
of "Thalassicollen Polycystinen, &c., des Mittelmeeres.")

7 & 8.—Spines or Spicules in Barbados deposit.

PLATE IX.

1.—Petalospiris foveolata—var. Ehr., (Mikrogeologie, Taf. XXXIV, 14.) .0075 high, spines included, .0031 dia. of ball.

2.—The same without the central spike through it.

3.—A Podocyrtis (?) of Ehrenberg.

4.—A Podocyrtis (?) nearly akin to Podocyrtis Ægles. (Mik. Taf. XXXV. B. 18); measures .0106 high, .0052 broad.

5.—A Podocyrtis (?) without the usual surmounting spine.

6.—A Lithomelissa (?) These beautiful little shapes, like crystal teapots or coffee-pots, for some primeval world's *Queen Mab*, are frequent in the Barbados deposit.

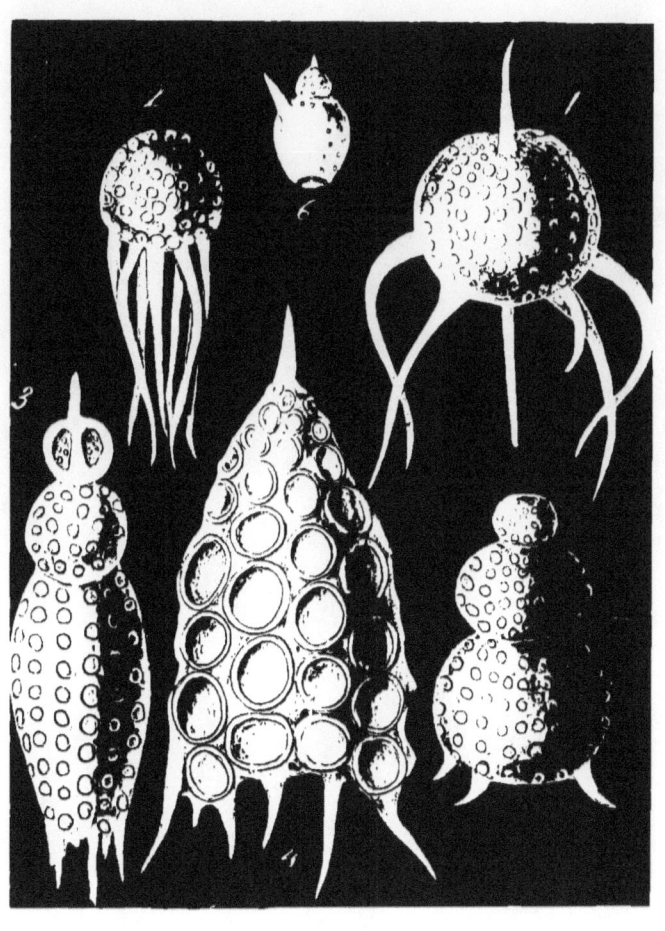

PLATE X.

FIG.

1.—Transparent cross, with tubular canals running through the arms and united by a central ring,—a structure resembling an object figured in Professor W. J. Bailey's "Microscopic forms in the Sea of Kamschatka," under the name "Spongolithes orthogona," but which he says he has referred with some hesitation to Spongolithis. Measures .01125 high, .008 broad, with a slightly warted or rugose surface.

2.—An Eucyrtidium form bearing tubular spinous projections, arranged in the pattern of the perforations in Eucyrtidium elegans; appears to be enclosed in a transparent egg-shaped sheath or envelope, .00362 long—Lithobotrys adspersa, Ehr. Mik. Taf. XXXVI, fig. 5, has the appearance of a wing or fin extending round the object in a somewhat similar way, and so has Carpocaninm solitarium, Taf. XXII, fig. 28. This specimen is in Slide No. 6½; Springfield, Barbados.

3.—Eucyrtidium (?) elegans, in an unconstricted state, .004 long, .0012 broad; 23 rows of nearly equi-distant perforations; from Chimborazo, Barbados.

4.—A Podocyrtis (?) mitra or papalis, var. (?) the lower part devoid of perforations, and with a thickening of the silex round the boundary of the plain part,—two spines from the apex.

5.—Podocyrtis papalis, Ehr. Mik. XXXVI, 23, .00687 high, .00375 broad. In numerous specimens the outline of the base varies considerably, but there always appears to be an internal ring or ledge.

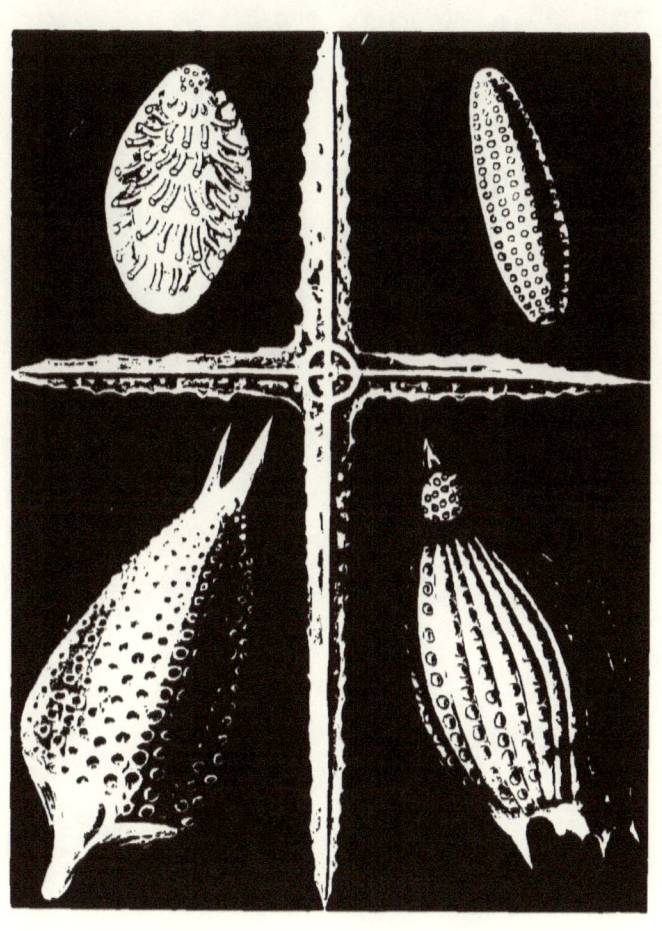

PLATE XI.

PLATE XII.

1:0.

1.—A spinous variety of Eucyrtidium ampullus (?) the narrow end prolonged into a tubulous spine,—diam. of bulb, .00275. Chimborazo, Barbados.

2.—Podocyrtis (?) whole height, .0112; breadth, .0055; height of cupola, .0027. Professor J. Müller says "in all the flask and bell-shaped Polycystins, the first joint *(glied)* of the reticulation begins from the top, and the number of the increasing links progresses with growth in a definite ratio." The links of the lower part in this fossil skeleton seem running into each other irregularly, like dropped stitches in a stocking, or bursting bubbles in a gelatinous film while solidifying.

3.—A further variation of Podocyrtis Schomburgkii, as shown on plate I, fig. 3.

4.—A modification of fig. 2, on plate I.

5 & 6.—The reticulations progressing further towards the "*Ladder*," or Lattice-shape. In fig. 6, the inner net is very plainly seen, its reticulations are also square, with quarter-inch magnifying power used, about 470 linear. Springfield, Barbados. In another slide is a broken-off top of one of these Ladder-Pyramids, with the narrow neck swelling out into the surmounting ball nucleus (?)

PLATE XIII.

FIG.

1 & 2.—Front and side view of a globose, slightly conical body, pretty
regularly areolated, and surrounded by a rounded honeycombed
ring. I am indebted to Dr. Greville for pointing out the front
view, as belonging to the same object, which he decided to be
"not a Diatom." Can it belong to Stephanopyxis or Xantho-
pyxis or some of that obscure group which even Ehrenberg
regards as "very doubtful Diatoms?" See Pritchard, page 827.
It is a very beautiful object, but difficult to get a good view of,
as the ring and the globe require different foci. In slide,
Vaughan's Barbados, No. 1; magnified about 400 diameters.

3.—Probably a variety of the Dictyospiris on Plate II, fig. 2, and Plate
XI, fig. 4, but with a greater number of spines, and differently
arranged.

4.—Possibly a Lychnocanium, with the apex dilated into a broad flat
spatula instead of the usual spine.

5.—A Rhabdolithes (?)

6.—A partially developed form spinning its outer web round the
nucleus, as in Müller's description of Haliomma.

7.—Chinese lantern shape in slide. Vaughan's resembles Dictyolithes
Pyramidalis of Mik., Pl. XX. fig. 30; but this is a much more
developed specimen.

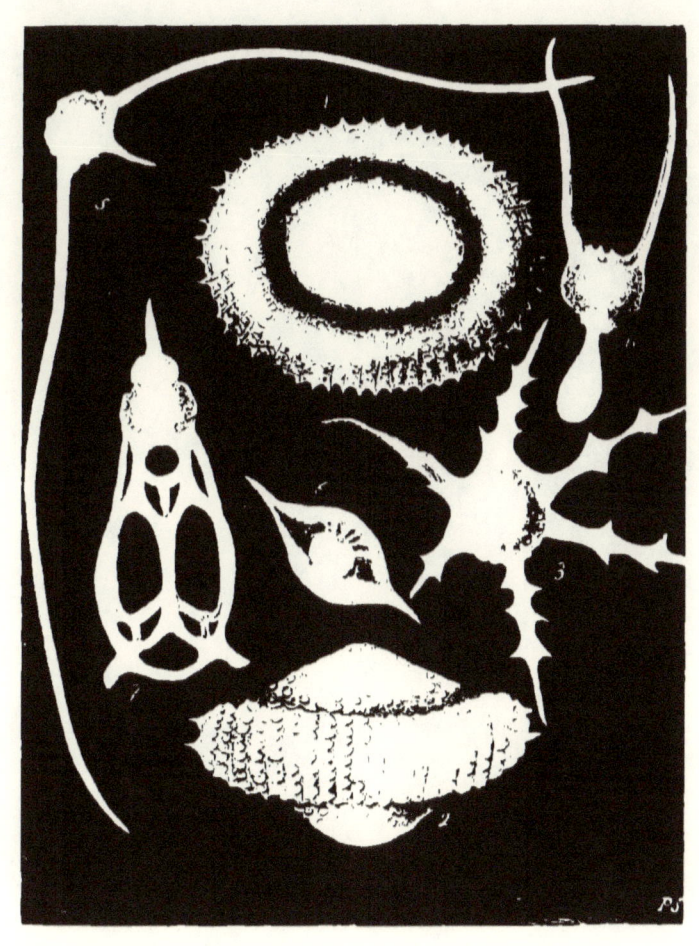

ד.
א.

PLATE XIV.

FIG.

1.—Astromma (?) A rhomboidal shaped mass of a very confused sponge-like web of fine tangled threads: inclosing in the middle a dark areolated ball. Four sharp spines protrude from the web at right angles, and measure from point to point ·01714.

2, 3, 4.—Varieties of Astromma Aristoteles (?)

5.—A more complete specimen of Rhopalastrum lagenosum. Mik. Pl. XXII, fig. 22.

6.- Central part of a similar organism. These beautiful crosses, with and without balls or spines at the ends of the arms, are very frequent in the deposit from Mt. Hillaby, Barbados. For the selected slides of that material from which the figures in this and the following plate are chiefly drawn, I am indebted to Geo Mansfield Browne Esq.

PLATE XV.

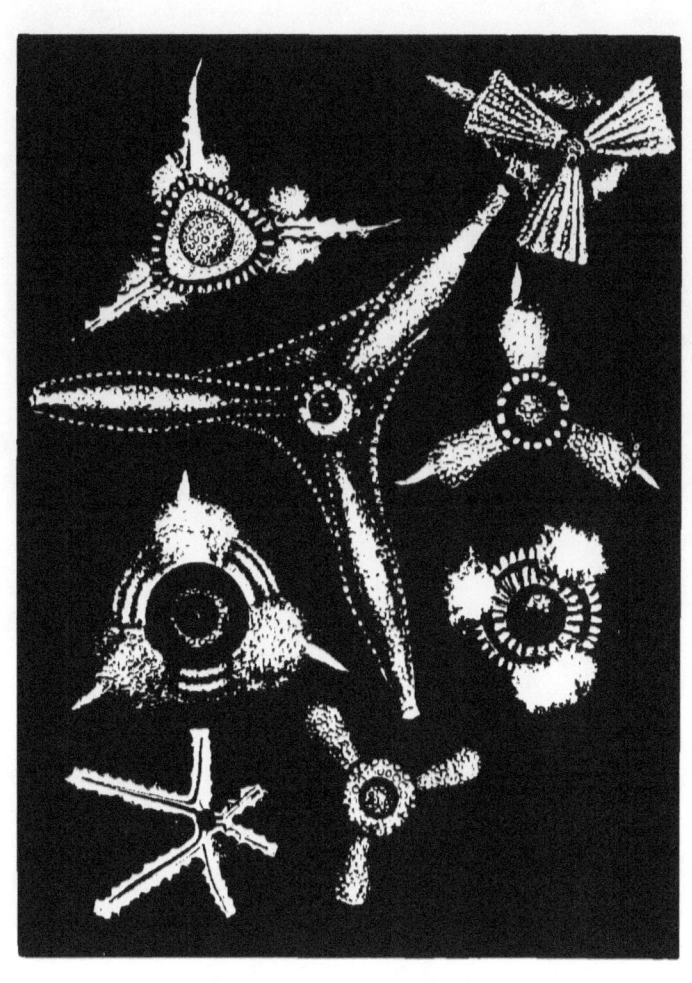

PLATE XVI.

FIG.

1.—A short hollow cylinder with large perforations, and ornamented with little pillars. In slide South Naparima, Trinidad, No. 5.

2 & 3.—Globular bodies with 2, or 3, or 4, pipe-like openings, the markings on them very irregular in size and distribution, and appear more like warts, or slight depressions, than actual punctures. Measure of diam. of bulb, about .0047. From South Naparima, Trinidad, No. 5.

4.—Obelisk pillar; resembles Professor Bailey's Rhizosolenia hebetata, which he found in Kamtskatka. This specimen is from Barbados.

5.—Two extraordinary long spines fixed by their small and branched ends to a very beautiful oval disk. Apparently the centre or axis of some large Polycystin in slide Barbados, No. 100$\frac{11}{33}$, measures from the centre to the point of one spine, .0228. Drawn as seen with half-inch objective.

6.—An elegant little transparent plate, without any perforations—a pretty crenate edge. In slide South Naparima, No. 2.

7.—A Haliomma (?) long, egg-shaped, very spinous and rough. Springfield, Barbados.

8.—The outer margin or circlet of Haliomma Humboldtii, shewing the points as extensions of the outer siliceous coat, and not attached to the radial spines or rafters.

Y
A

PLATE XVII.

PLATE XVIII.

FIG.

1.—*A rough spongelike-looking ball with strong spines.*

2.—*Spongolithis (?) a spicule.*

3.—A state of a Haliomma—strong spokes from central nucleus to circumference, at unequal distances—some network apparently spinning partly over one side, according to Müller's description.

4.—*Spongolithis anchora of Ehrenberg—A spicule.*

5.—*Spongolithis ramosa, Ehr.*

6.—*Serpent-like form—very frequent and variable in the Barbados deposit.*

7.—*Lithasteriscus reniformis. Ehr., "Nord and Sud Amerika," Taf. VI. fig. 35. I think all these bean-like forms are warted or roughened on the surface, not truly foraminated.*

8.—An irregular three-lobed transparent Plate from Chimborazo, Barbados, analogous to fig. 6 on Pl. VII. Dr. Wallich says these are *parts* of an organism constituting a new genus intermediate between Sponges and Polycystins: this plate, forming part of the *outer* siliceous skeleton, the interior being filled with free spicules. The ovals, Nos. 1 and 2, on Pl. 7, (of which many more examples have since been found) are *plates instead of spicules,* taking the place of an *internal* skeleton of a kind of organism of which no perfect specimen has yet been found; and which is also intermediate between Sponges and Polycystins.

9.—Spongolithis aspera.

PLATE XIX.

FIG.
1.—9.—Probably varieties of the same species of Polycystin in the Barbados deposit. They frequently assume a triangular appearance, there are no wide external openings visible,—but Dr. Wallich has detected small openings, which he compares to a "Cat's claw," at the roots of the spines.

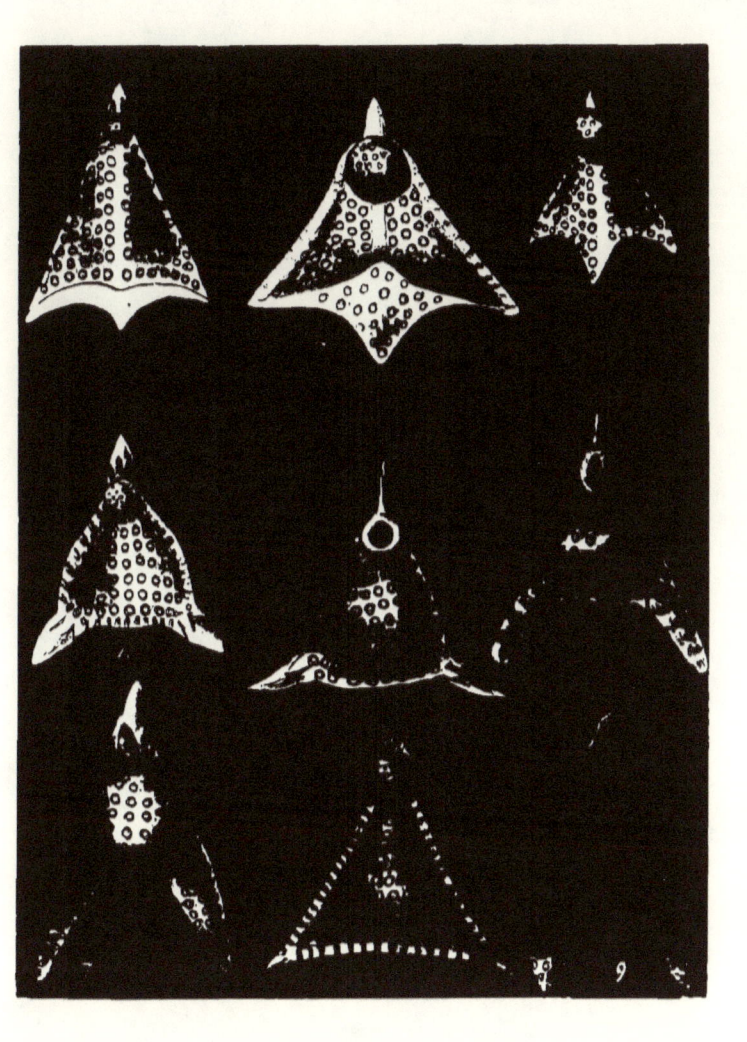

٢
٣٧
٨

PLATE XX.

PLATE XXI.

FIG.

1.—A transparent flat branch—with canals, but no perforations—as seen with half-inch objective: in slide, Chimborazo, No. 4.

2.—A six-sided cushion, still a Stephanastrum.

3.—Stylosphæra of Ehrenberg; rather dwarfed, and one spine become bifid.

4.—Many-spined Haliomma?

5.—A Polycystin, not unfrequent in Barbados earth.

6.—A massive beautiful spine, looks as if it might have been the central support of some organism.

7.—Again one of these Plate-spicules—of what? Dr. Greville suggested, July, 1863, that it might probably be Actiniscus stella; Professor Bailey considered Actiniscus as a Polycystin.

8.—A fenestrated Pyramid, possibly a Podocyrtis; similar to figs. 5 and 6 on plate 12, but with this remarkable difference, that the bars, or network of silex bounding the window-like openings, appear to be very finely perforated or cellulated. Dr. Wallich examined this specimen, and considered that the roughened, or apparently cellular appearance, might have arisen from a diseased state of the sarcode while depositing the siliceous bars. I have noticed the same appearance on parts of other specimens, and on spines which have become bulbous at the ends. No inner web discernible through these windows.

9 & 10.—Beautiful little siliceous stars. Cambridge, Barbados.

11.—An extraordinary *silicified* cast of the septal lines and primordial segment, with part of the interior of a Textilaria; in a slide from Springfield, Barbados. Dr. Davy. That the original *carbonate* is changed to *silex* is proved, not only by its having resisted the treatment with strong acids and alkalis used in preparing the Barbados earths for the microscope, but also that no colour was shewn under the strong Polarizing apparatus of powerful microscopes; and the process of such a change is perfectly explained by Professor Ehrenberg's account of the infiltration of silicate of iron into some of the Foraminifera, giving thus perfectly preserved casts of the inside of the shells[a]; this specimen measures .0131 in length.

* Note. "Ueber den Grünsand, und seine Erlauterung." Berlin, 1856.

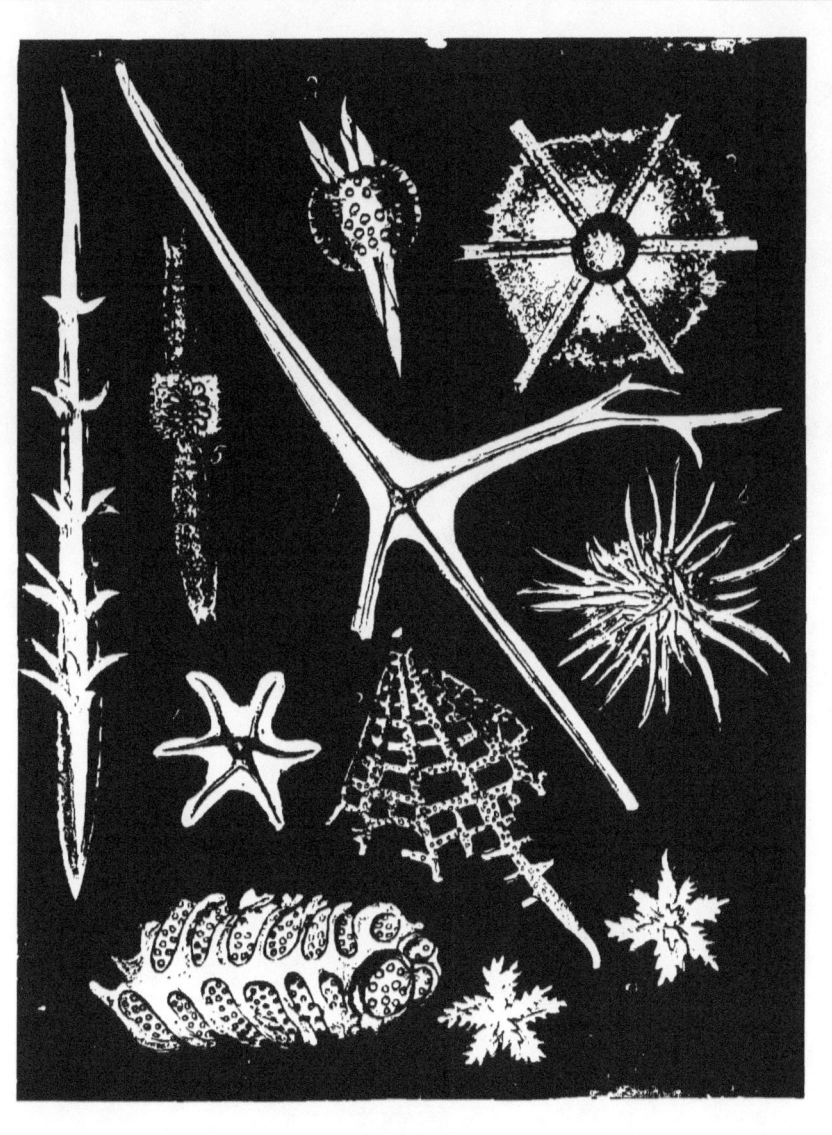

٢
د

PLATE XXII.

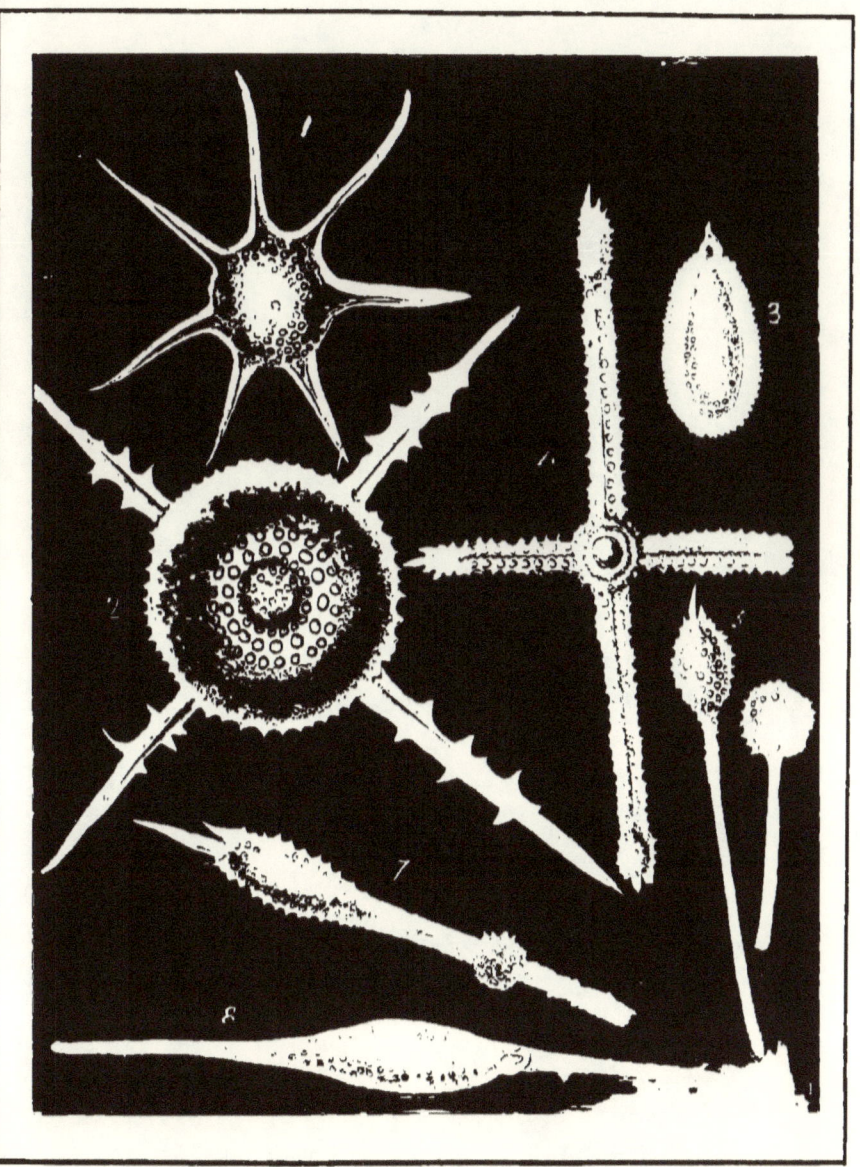

TY
A

PLATE XXIII.

FIG.

1.—A Stephanastrum, with the four central arms similar to those of Stephanastrum rhombus of Ehrenberg, enveloped in a *circular* spongiose web, beyond which extends an irregularly-spinous transparent siliceous border, which also extends round the ends of the arms. I think this round web is the normal form of the Stephanastrums and Rhopalastrums, and the key to all the curious 3, 4, 5, and 6-sided cushions; the number of arms deciding the number of sides, and stretching out the web in the course of growth into the various shapes as long as it remains attached to them; in slide "Chimborazo Barbados Rd," size .0228.

2.—Resembles Placolithes radiata. Mikrogeologie Pl. XXXIV, fig. 5. There are two valves, the upper one plaited like a fan. I have since seen a broken specimen, in which the plaits appear like tubes, hollow, like the beautiful raised ribs on the African Cardium costatum. Dr. Wallich confirmed the notion of the fan-like plaits, by detecting a crack across one of them.

3.—A lovely transparent cross, with doubly trifid ends, possibly a sponge spicule; in form most nearly resembling some of the spicules of Hyalonema mirabilis, on Taf. III. of Professor Max Schultze's "Beitrage," &c.

4.—A transparent Plate, irregularly three-lobed, each lobe bifurcate, in slide "S.P. Barbados." Material from Dr. Kingsley. It appears to be of the nature of those "Hex-radiate plate-spicules" depicted by Dr. Bowerbank as from a "Euplectella."

5.—An explanation of mode of growth of fig. 5 on Pl. VII. A Dictyochus net?

6.—A Rhabdolithes, giving a curious example of the way the siliceous outshooting spines seem to go wandering on wherever they find the least obstruction; at '*a*' there seems to have been an intended change of course, checked. The extreme flexibility of these spines might lead to a supposition whether there might not be combined with the silex in their composition some portion of the keratode (or horny matter) stated by Dr. Bowerbank to enter into the formation of even the siliceous coating of the spines.

7.—A double circlet of Acanthodesmia of Müller. A single circlet is given on Pl. II, fig. 6. Barbados earth.

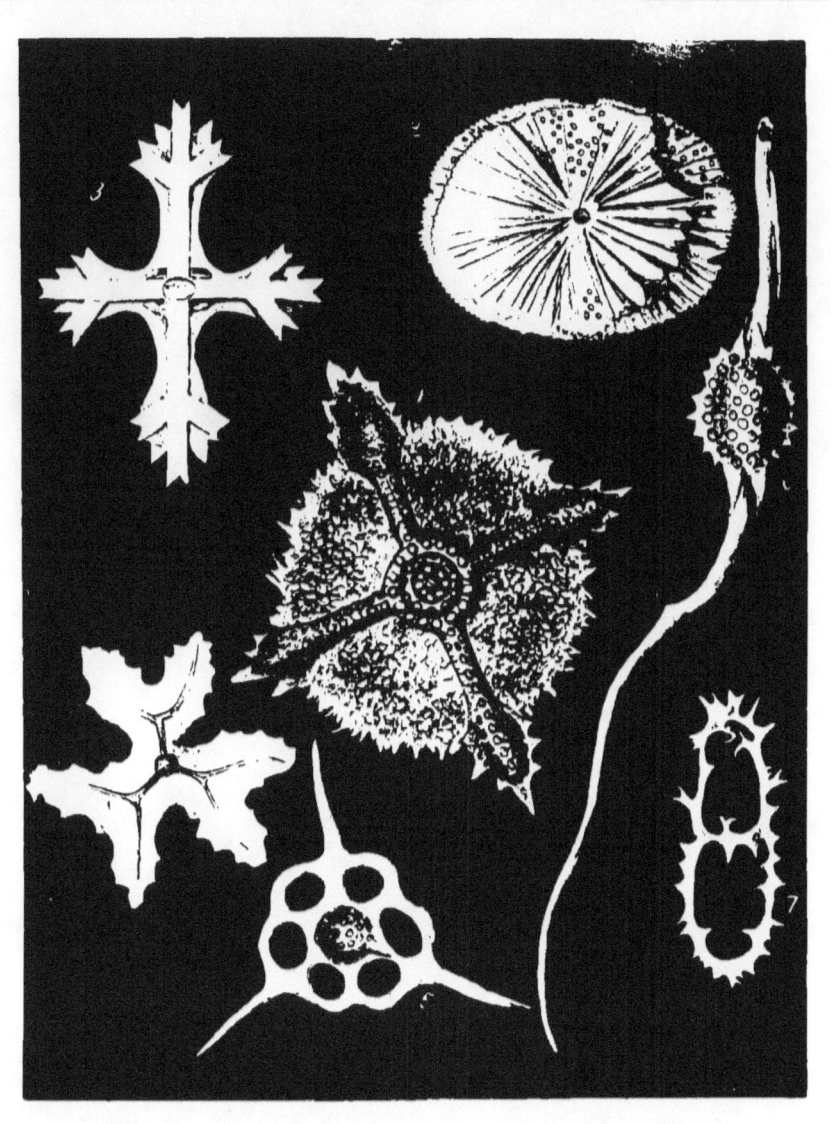

٢٧
ھ

PLATE XXIV.

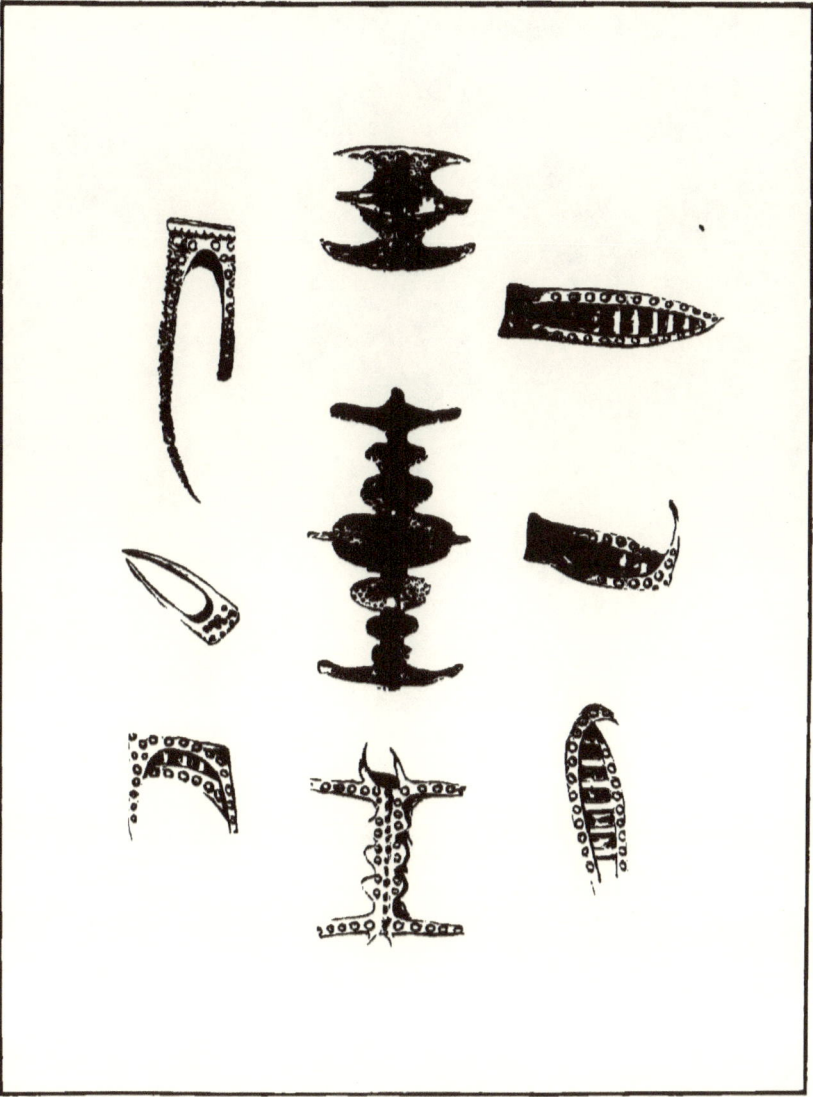

www.ingramcontent.com/pod-product-compliance
Lightning Source LLC
Chambersburg PA
CBHW032151010726
47493CB00008BA/2657